THIS BOOK *should*

BELONGS TO:

....

....

A Very Naughty Rabbit

A Very Naughty Rabbit

Tales of Mayhem and Mischief

WARNE

FREDERICK WARNE

Published by the Penguin Group
Penguin Books Ltd, 80 Strand, London WC2R 0RL, England
Penguin Group (USA) Inc., 375 Hudson Street, New York, New York 10014, USA
Penguin Books Australia Ltd, 250 Camberwell Road, Camberwell, Victoria 3124, Australia
Penguin Books Canada Ltd, 90 Eglinton Avenue East, Suite 700, Toronto, Ontario, Canada M4P 2Y3
Penguin Books India (P) Ltd, 11 Community Centre, Panchsheel Park, New Delhi 110 017, India
Penguin Books (NZ) Ltd, 67 Apollo Drive, Rosedale, North Shore 0632, New Zealand
Penguin Books (South Africa) (Pty) Ltd, 24 Sturdee Avenue, Rosebank, Johannesburg 2196, South Africa

Penguin Books Ltd, Registered Offices: 80 Strand, London WC2R 0RL, England

Web site at: www.peterrabbit.com

First published by Frederick Warne 2010
1 3 5 7 9 10 8 6 4 2

ISBN 978-0-7232-6589-4

Color reproduction by MDP (Media, Development and Printing Ltd.)
Printed and bound in China

CONTENTS

ABOUT BEATRIX POTTER

Beatrix Potter was born in London in 1866, and like all upper-class Victorian children, she was expected to be a model of good behaviour. "Children should be seen and not heard," was a favourite maxim of those days, and Beatrix was an obedient and well-behaved daughter. But she could still create the fun of being naughty in her imagination. She loved the *Uncle Remus* stories about the trickster Brer Rabbit. She also kept pets of her own in the schoolroom of her house and recognized that dogs, rabbits and mice had much more leeway than she did to indulge in mischief.

Beatrix Potter grew up to be a talented writer and artist. In 1893 she sent an illustrated letter to her friend's five-year-old son, Noel Moore, which described the adventures of a rabbit called Peter who disobeyed his mother and ran away into Mr. McGregor's garden. Several years later Beatrix decided to turn this letter into a little book – *The Tale of Peter Rabbit*. It was an instant bestseller when it was published in 1902. Thousands of children enjoyed the tale of naughty Peter just as much as Noel, the first reader, had done. Crime never pays in her stories, but Beatrix understood the charm of breaking the rules. When her publisher's daughter complained that she thought Peter was too good and she wanted a story about a really naughty rabbit, Beatrix obliged with *The Story of A Fierce Bad Rabbit*, featuring the most badly behaved character of all.

As Beatrix became established as a successful author she was able to use her money to buy property in the Lake District. In 1913 she married a Cumbrian solicitor, William Heelis, and for the last thirty years of her life she enjoyed a second career as a farmer and sheep-breeder. In her later years she was to develop some sympathy with Mr. McGregor, when mischief-making local children trespassed on her land and stole apples from her orchard. But her stories of Peter and his friends "kept on their way", as she put it, and a century later still remain a constant inspiration to the rebellious spirit.

THE TALE OF
PETER RABBIT

or

A VERY Naughty Rabbit

ABOUT THIS BOOK

The story of naughty Peter Rabbit in Mr. McGregor's garden first appeared in a picture letter Beatrix Potter wrote to Noel Moore, the young son of her former governess, in 1893. Encouraged by her success in having some greetings card designs published, Beatrix remembered the letter seven years later, and expanded it into a little picture book, with black-and-white illustrations. It was rejected by several publishers, so Beatrix had it printed herself, to give to family and friends.

About this time, Frederick Warne agreed to publish the tale if the author would supply color pictures, and the book finally appeared in 1902, priced at one shilling (5p or 7 cents). It was an instant success, and has remained so ever since. It has a pacy story with an engaging hero, an exciting chase and a happy ending, matched with exquisite illustrations, and the result is a children's classic whose appeal is ageless.

ONCE UPON A TIME there were four little Rabbits, and their names were —

Flopsy,
Mopsy,
Cotton-tail,
and Peter.

They lived with their Mother in a sand-bank, underneath the root of a very big fir-tree.

"Now, my dears," said old Mrs. Rabbit one morning, "you may go into the fields or down the lane, but don't go into Mr. McGregor's garden.

"Your Father had an accident there; he was put in a pie by Mrs. McGregor.

"Now run along, and don't get into mischief. I am going out."

Then old Mrs. Rabbit took a basket and her umbrella, and went through the wood to the baker's. She bought a loaf of brown bread and five currant buns.

Flopsy, Mopsy and Cotton-tail, who were good little bunnies, went down the lane to gather blackberries;

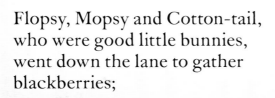

But Peter, who was very naughty, ran straight away to Mr. McGregor's garden,

And squeezed under the gate!

First he ate some lettuces and some French beans; and then he ate some radishes;

And then, feeling rather
sick, he went to look for
some parsley.

But round the end of a
cucumber frame, whom should
he meet but Mr. McGregor!

Mr. McGregor was on his hands
and knees planting out young
cabbages, but he jumped up and
ran after Peter, waving a rake
and calling out, "Stop thief!"

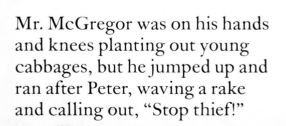

Peter was most dreadfully frightened; he rushed all over the garden, for he had forgotten the way back to the gate. He lost one of his shoes among the cabbages,

And the other shoe amongst the potatoes.

After losing them, he ran on four legs and went faster, so that I think he might have got away altogether if he had not unfortunately run into a gooseberry net, and got caught by the large buttons on his jacket. It was a blue jacket with brass buttons, quite new.

Peter gave himself up for lost, and shed big tears; but his sobs were overheard by some friendly sparrows, who flew to him in great excitement, and implored him to exert himself.

Mr. McGregor came up with a sieve, which he intended to pop upon the top of Peter; but Peter wriggled out just in time, leaving his jacket behind him,

And rushed into the tool-shed, and jumped into a can. It would have been a beautiful thing to hide in, if it had not had so much water in it.

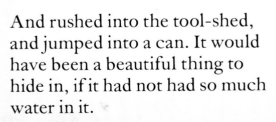

Mr. McGregor was quite sure that Peter was somewhere in the tool-shed, perhaps hidden underneath a flower-pot. He began to turn them over carefully, looking under each.

Presently Peter sneezed — "Kertyschoo!" Mr. McGregor was after him in no time,

And tried to put his foot upon Peter, who jumped out of a window, upsetting three plants. The window was too small for Mr. McGregor, and he was tired of running after Peter. He went back to his work.

Peter sat down to rest; he was out of breath and trembling with fright, and he had not the least idea which way to go. Also he was very damp with sitting in that can.

After a time he began to wander about, going lippity — lippity — not very fast, and looking all round.

He found a door in a wall; but it was locked, and there was no room for a fat little rabbit to squeeze underneath.

An old mouse was running in and out over the stone door-step, carrying peas and beans to her family in the wood. Peter asked her the way to the gate, but she had such a large pea in her mouth that she could not answer. She only shook her head at him. Peter began to cry.

Then he tried to find his way straight across the garden, but he became more and more puzzled. Presently, he came to a pond where Mr. McGregor filled his water-cans. A white cat was staring at some gold-fish; she sat very, very still, but now and then the tip of her tail twitched as if it were alive. Peter thought it best to go away without speaking to her; he had heard about cats from his cousin, little Benjamin Bunny.

He went back towards the
tool-shed, but suddenly, quite
close to him, he heard the noise
of a hoe — scr-r-ritch, scratch,
scratch, scritch. Peter scuttered
underneath the bushes.

But presently, as nothing happened,
he came out, and climbed upon
a wheelbarrow, and peeped over.
The first thing he saw was
Mr. McGregor hoeing onions.
His back was turned towards Peter,
and beyond him was the gate!

Peter got down very quietly off
the wheelbarrow, and started
running as fast as he could go,
along a straight walk behind
some black-currant bushes.

Mr. McGregor caught sight of
him at the corner, but Peter did
not care. He slipped underneath
the gate, and was safe at last in
the wood outside the garden.

Mr. McGregor hung up the little jacket and the shoes for a scarecrow to frighten the blackbirds.

Peter never stopped running or looked behind him till he got home to the big fir-tree.

He was so tired that he flopped down upon the nice soft sand on the floor of the rabbit-hole, and shut his eyes. His mother was busy cooking; she wondered what he had done with his clothes. It was the second little jacket and pair of shoes that Peter had lost in a fortnight!

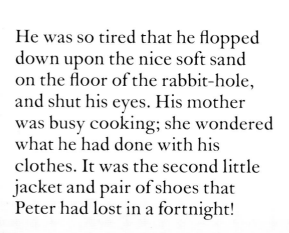

I am sorry to say that Peter was not very well during the evening.

His mother put him to bed, and made some camomile tea; and she gave a dose of it to Peter!

"One table-spoonful to be taken at bed-time."

But Flopsy, Mopsy, and Cotton-tail had bread and milk and blackberries for supper.

The End.

Not quite. Can you believe what that brazen rabbit did next? Read on . . .

Mr. McGregor,
Gardener's Cottage.

Dear Sir,
I write to ask whether your spring cabbages are ready? Kindly reply by return and oblige.

Yrs. truly,
Peter Rabbit.

Master P. Rabbit,
Under Fir Tree.

Sir,
I rite by desir of my Husband Mr. McGregor who is in Bedd with a Cauld to say if you Comes heer agane we will inform the Polisse.

Jane McGregor.

P.S. I have bort a new Py-Dish, itt is vary large.

TAKE HEED!

*W*ell, what can we learn from this sorry tale? Poor, frightened Peter lies unwell in his bed, having lost his dear little jacket and shoes to a scarecrow. To make things worse, he has missed out on a delicious supper! It just goes to show that children – whether human or rabbit – should <u>ALWAYS</u> listen to their parents.

Greedy Peter, so tempted by Mr. McGregor's tasty vegetables, ignored his mother's advice. He was very lucky not to end up in a pie like his father, don't you think?

After such a scare, one would have expected the naughty rabbit to stay close to home. So you will be shocked to discover that Peter ventured back into Mr. McGregor's garden soon afterwards! He was not alone, however, but accompanied by his equally mischievous little cousin, Benjamin Bunny . . .

THE TALE OF
BENJAMIN BUNNY
or
The Fate of the Reckless Rabbit

ABOUT THIS BOOK

The real-life Benjamin Bunny was a tame rabbit of Beatrix Potter's, whom she sketched constantly, and whose exploits continually amused her. "He is an abject coward, but believes in bluster, could stare our old dog out of countenance, chase a cat that has turned tail." Although Benjamin had died by 1904, when this story was published, Beatrix may well have been thinking of him when she created Peter Rabbit's cousin, Benjamin. Little Benjamin is a very self-possessed animal, who makes himself quite at home in Mr. McGregor's garden.

Beatrix sketched background scenes for the tale while on holiday at Fawe Park, a house with a beautiful garden in the Lake District. The book is dedicated to "the children of Sawrey from Old Mr. Bunny". Beatrix was later to settle in the Lake District village of Sawrey, buying a small farm there in 1905.

ONE MORNING a little rabbit sat on a bank. He pricked his ears and listened to the trit-trot, trit-trot of a pony.

A gig was coming along the road; it was driven by Mr. McGregor, and beside him sat Mrs. McGregor in her best bonnet.

As soon as they had passed, little Benjamin Bunny slid down into the road, and set off — with a hop, skip and a jump — to call upon his relations, who lived in the wood at the back of Mr. McGregor's garden.

That wood was full of rabbit-holes; and in the neatest sandiest hole of all, lived Benjamin's aunt and his cousins — Flopsy, Mopsy, Cotton-tail and Peter.

Old Mrs. Rabbit was a widow; she earned her living by knitting rabbit-wool mittens and muffetees (I once bought a pair at a bazaar). She also sold herbs, and rosemary tea, and rabbit-tobacco (which is what *we* call lavender).

Little Benjamin did not very much want to see his Aunt.

He came round the back of the fir-tree, and nearly tumbled upon the top of his Cousin Peter.

Peter was sitting by himself. He looked poorly, and was dressed in a red cotton pocket-handkerchief.

"Peter," — said little Benjamin, in a whisper — "who has got your clothes?"

Peter replied — "The scarecrow in Mr. McGregor's garden," and described how he had been chased about the garden, and had dropped his shoes and coat.

Little Benjamin sat down beside his cousin, and assured him that Mr. McGregor had gone out in a gig, and Mrs. McGregor also; and certainly for the day, because she was wearing her best bonnet.

Peter said he hoped that it would rain.

At this point, old Mrs. Rabbit's voice was heard inside the rabbit-hole, calling — "Cotton-tail! Cotton-tail! fetch some more camomile!"

Peter said he thought he might feel better if he went for a walk.

They went away hand in hand, and got upon the flat top of the wall at the bottom of the wood. From here they looked down into Mr. McGregor's garden. Peter's coat and shoes were plainly to be seen upon the scarecrow, topped with an old tam-o-shanter of Mr. McGregor's.

Little Benjamin said, "It spoils people's clothes to squeeze under a gate; the proper way to get in, is to climb down a pear tree."

Peter fell down head first; but it was of no consequence, as the bed below was newly raked and quite soft.

It had been sown with lettuces.

They left a great many odd little foot-marks all over the bed, especially little Benjamin, who was wearing clogs.

Little Benjamin said that the first thing to be done was to get back Peter's clothes, in order that they might be able to use the pocket-handkerchief.

They took them off the scarecrow. There had been rain during the night; there was water in the shoes, and the coat was somewhat shrunk.

Benjamin tried on the tam-o-shanter, but it was too big for him.

Then he suggested that they should fill the pocket-handkerchief with onions, as a little present for his Aunt.

Peter did not seem to be enjoying himself; he kept hearing noises.

Benjamin, on the contrary, was perfectly at home, and ate a lettuce leaf. He said that he was in the habit of coming to the garden with his father to get lettuces for their Sunday dinner.

(The name of little Benjamin's papa was old Mr. Benjamin Bunny.)

The lettuces certainly were very fine.

Peter did not eat anything; he said he should like to go home. Presently he dropped half the onions.

Little Benjamin said that it was not possible to get back up the pear tree, with a load of vegetables. He led the way boldly towards the other end of the garden. They went along a little walk on planks, under a sunny red-brick wall.

The mice sat on their door-steps cracking cherry-stones; they winked at Peter Rabbit and little Benjamin Bunny.

Presently Peter let the
pocket-handkerchief
go again.

They got amongst
flower-pots, and frames
and tubs; Peter heard
noises worse than ever,
his eyes were as big as
lolly-pops!

He was a step or two in
front of his cousin, when
he suddenly stopped.

This is what those little rabbits saw round that corner!

Little Benjamin took one look, and then, in half a minute less than no time, he hid himself and Peter and the onions underneath a large basket . . .

The cat got up and stretched herself, and came and sniffed at the basket.

Perhaps she liked the smell of onions!

Anyway, she sat down upon the top of the basket.

She sat there for *five hours*.

*

I cannot draw you a picture
of Peter and Benjamin
underneath the basket,
because it was quite dark,
and because the smell of
onions was fearful; it made
Peter Rabbit and little
Benjamin cry.

The sun got round behind the wood, and it was quite late in the
afternoon; but still the cat sat upon the basket.

At length there was a
pitter-patter, pitter-patter,
and some bits of mortar
fell from the wall above.

The cat looked up and
saw old Mr. Benjamin
Bunny prancing along
the top of the wall of the
upper terrace.

He was smoking a pipe
of rabbit-tobacco, and had
a little switch in his hand.

He was looking for his son.

Old Mr. Bunny had no opinion whatever of cats.

He took a tremendous jump off the top of the wall on to the top of the cat, and cuffed it off the basket, and kicked it into the green-house, scratching off a handful of fur.

The cat was too much surprised to scratch back.

When old Mr. Bunny had driven the cat into the green-house, he locked the door.

Then he came back to the basket and took out his son Benjamin by the ears, and whipped him with the little switch.

Then he took out his nephew Peter.

Then he took out the handkerchief of onions, and marched out of the garden.

When Mr. McGregor returned about half an hour later, he observed several things which perplexed him.

It looked as though some person had been walking all over the garden in a pair of clogs — only the foot-marks were too ridiculously little!

Also he could not understand how the cat could have managed to shut herself up *inside* the green-house, locking the door upon the *outside*.

When Peter got home, his mother forgave him, because she was so glad to see that he had found his shoes and coat. Cotton-tail and Peter folded up the pocket-handkerchief, and old Mrs. Rabbit strung up the onions and hung them from the kitchen ceiling, with the bunches of herbs and the rabbit-tobacco.

The End?
Well, it would have been . . .

. . . if peter hadn't written <u>another</u> of his letters!

Master Benjamin Bunny,
The Warren.

Dear Cousin Benjamin,

I have had a very ill written letter
from Mrs. McGregor she says Mr. M.
is in bed with a cold will you meet
me at the corner of the wood near
their garden at 6 this evening?
In haste.

Yr. aff. cousin,
Peter Rabbit

Oh, foolish Benjamin Bunny! Having seen the McGregors leaving the house, he was so sure that he and Peter would not be caught! He forgot that there are other rabbit enemies – not only human ones – lurking in the garden . . .

Still, you must agree that the unlucky bunnies were punished for their mischief. To be trapped for five hours by a disagreeable cat is bad enough; to be trapped in darkness with the smell of stinking onions quite dreadful! Luckily for the tearful bunnies, Benjamin's father turned up to save them. But unluckily for his young son, Old Mr. Bunny proceeded to whip him thoroughly!

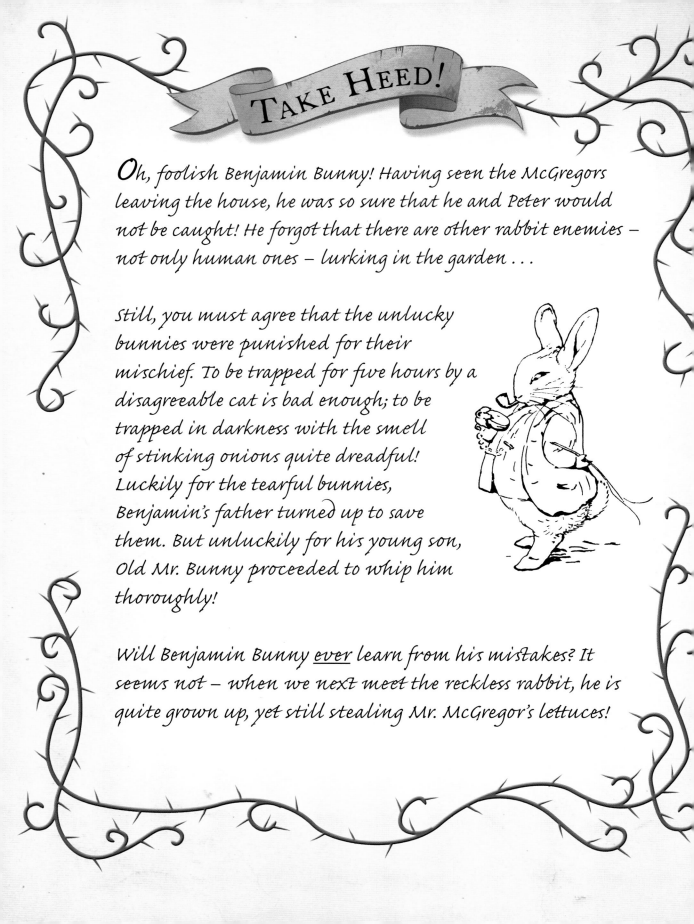

Will Benjamin Bunny <u>ever</u> learn from his mistakes? It seems not – when we next meet the reckless rabbit, he is quite grown up, yet still stealing Mr. McGregor's lettuces!

THE TALE OF
THE FLOPSY BUNNIES

or

The Perils of Eating Too Much Lettuce

ABOUT THIS BOOK

The Tale of The Flopsy Bunnies pays another visit to the world of Peter Rabbit and Benjamin Bunny. Both rabbits have now grown up, Benjamin has married Peter's sister Flopsy and although still "improvident and cheerful", has a large family to care for. Beatrix Potter was well aware that her earlier books had created a huge demand for rabbit stories, and dedicated this one, "For all little friends of Mr. McGregor and Peter and Benjamin". Besides, she enjoyed painting rabbits, and gardens too. When preparing the book in 1909 she was staying with her uncle Fred and aunt Harriet Burton at Gwaynynog, their large house in Wales, and made many studies of the garden there. She described it on an earlier visit as "the prettiest kind of garden, where bright old-fashioned flowers grow amongst the currant bushes". It is beautifully depicted in her lovely illustrations.

IT IS SAID that the effect of eating too much lettuce is "soporific".

I have never felt sleepy after eating lettuces; but then *I* am not a rabbit.

They certainly had a very soporific effect upon the Flopsy Bunnies!

When Benjamin Bunny grew up, he married his Cousin Flopsy. They had a large family, and they were very improvident and cheerful.

I do not remember the separate names of their children; they were generally called the "Flopsy Bunnies".

As there was not always quite enough to eat — Benjamin used to borrow cabbages from Flopsy's brother, Peter Rabbit, who kept a nursery garden.

Sometimes Peter Rabbit had no cabbages to spare.

When this happened, the Flopsy Bunnies went across the field to a rubbish heap, in the ditch outside Mr. McGregor's garden.

Mr. McGregor's rubbish heap was a mixture. There were jam pots and paper bags, and mountains of chopped grass from the mowing machine (which always tasted oily), and some rotten vegetable marrows and an old boot or two. One day — oh joy! — there were a quantity of overgrown lettuces, which had "shot" into flower.

The Flopsy Bunnies simply stuffed lettuces. By degrees, one after another, they were overcome with slumber, and lay down in the mown grass.

Benjamin was not so much overcome as his children. Before going to sleep he was sufficiently wide awake to put a paper bag over his head to keep off the flies.

The little Flopsy Bunnies slept delightfully in the warm sun. From the lawn beyond the garden came the distant clacketty sound of the mowing machine. The bluebottles buzzed about the wall, and a little old mouse picked over the rubbish among the jam pots.

(I can tell you her name, she was called Thomasina Tittlemouse, a wood-mouse with a long tail.)

She rustled across the paper bag, and awakened Benjamin Bunny.

The mouse apologized profusely, and said that she knew Peter Rabbit.

While she and Benjamin were
talking, close under the wall,
they heard a heavy tread above
their heads; and suddenly
Mr. McGregor emptied out a
sackful of lawn mowings right
upon the top of the sleeping
Flopsy Bunnies! Benjamin shrank
down under his paper bag.
The mouse hid in a jam pot.

The little rabbits smiled sweetly
in their sleep under the shower of
grass; they did not awake because
the lettuces had been so soporific.

They dreamt that their mother
Flopsy was tucking them up in a
hay bed.

Mr. McGregor looked down
after emptying his sack. He saw
some funny little brown tips of
ears sticking up through the lawn
mowings. He stared at them for
some time.

Presently a fly settled on one of them and it moved.

Mr. McGregor climbed down on to the rubbish heap —

"One, two, three, four! five! six leetle rabbits!" said he as
he dropped them into his sack.

The Flopsy Bunnies dreamt
that their mother was turning
them over in bed. They stirred a
little in their sleep, but still they
did not wake up.

Mr. McGregor tied up the sack
and left it on the wall.

He went to put away the
mowing machine.

While he was gone, Mrs. Flopsy
Bunny (who had remained at
home) came across the field.

She looked suspiciously at
the sack and wondered where
everybody was?

Then the mouse came out of her jam pot, and Benjamin took the paper bag off his head, and they told the doleful tale.

Benjamin and Flopsy were in despair, they could not undo the string.

But Mrs. Tittlemouse was a resourceful person. She nibbled a hole in the bottom corner of the sack.

The little rabbits were pulled out and pinched to wake them.

Their parents stuffed the empty sack with three rotten vegetable marrows, an old blacking-brush and two decayed turnips.

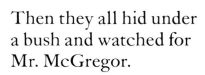

Then they all hid under a bush and watched for Mr. McGregor.

Mr. McGregor came back and
picked up the sack, and carried
it off.

He carried it hanging down,
as if it were rather heavy.

The Flopsy Bunnies followed
at a safe distance.

They watched him go into
his house.

And then they crept up to the
window to listen.

Mr. McGregor threw down
the sack on the stone floor in
a way that would have been
extremely painful to the Flopsy
Bunnies, if they had happened
to have been inside it.

They could hear him drag his chair on the flags, and chuckle —

"One, two, three, four, five, six leetle rabbits!" said Mr. McGregor.

"Eh? What's that? What have they been spoiling now?" enquired Mrs. McGregor.

"One, two, three, four, five, six leetle fat rabbits!" repeated Mr. McGregor, counting on his fingers — "one, two, three —"

"Don't you be silly; what do you mean, you silly old man?"

"In the sack! one, two, three, four, five, six!" replied Mr. McGregor.

(The youngest Flopsy Bunny got upon the window-sill.)

Mrs. McGregor took hold of the sack and felt it. She said she could feel six, but they must be *old* rabbits, because they were so hard and all different shapes.

"Not fit to eat; but the skins will do fine to line my old cloak."

"Line your old cloak?" shouted Mr. McGregor — "I shall sell them and buy myself baccy!"

"Rabbit tobacco! I shall skin them and cut off their heads."

Mrs. McGregor untied the
sack and put her hand inside.
    When she felt the vegetables
she became very very angry.
She said that Mr. McGregor
had "done it a purpose".

And Mr. McGregor was very
angry too. One of the rotten
marrows came flying through
the kitchen window, and hit the
youngest Flopsy Bunny.
    It was rather hurt.

Then Benjamin and Flopsy
thought that it was time to
go home.

So Mr. McGregor did not get his tobacco, and Mrs. McGregor did not get her rabbit skins.

But next Christmas Thomasina Tittlemouse got a present of enough rabbit-wool to make herself a cloak and a hood, and a handsome muff and a pair of warm mittens.

The End . . .

. . . of the story, but thankfully not the end of the bunnies!

Let's see what became of them . . .

Miss M. Moller,
Caldecote Grange,
Biggleswade.

My dear Miss Moller,
I am pleased to hear that you like the
F. Bunnies, because some people do think
there has been too much bunnies; and there
is going to be some more!
My family will appear again in the next book;
and Cottontail is put in because you asked
after her, which me and Cottontail thanks you
for kind inquiries and remembrance.

Yrs. respectful
Flopsy Bunny.

Dear Madam
My wife Mrs. Flopsy Bunny
has replied to your inquiries,
because Miss potter will
attend to nothing but hatching
spring chickens; there is
another hatch chirping this
evening. And she is supposed
to be doing a Book, about us
and the Fox; but she does
not get on; neither has she
answered all her xmas
letters yet.

Yrs
B. Bunny.

Master John Hough,
88 Darenth Road,
N.W.

Dear Master John Hough,
I and my Family (6) are writing to
you because Miss Potter has got no
stamps left and she has got a cold,
we think Miss Potter is lazy. I think
you are a fine big boy; my children
are small rabbits at present.

Yrs. respectfully,
Mrs. Flopsy Bunny.

Dear Master
John Hough,
I wish you a Merry
Christmas! I am going
to have an apple for my
Christmas dinner & some
celery tops. The cabbages
are all frosted but there
is lots of hay.

Yrs. aff.
First Flopsy Bunny.
XXXXXXX

Dear Master
John,
I wish you the
same as my
eldest brother,
and I am going to
have the same
dinner.

Yrs. aff.
2nd. Flopsy Bunny.
xxxxxx

Dear Master Hough,
I wish you the
compliments of the
season. We have got
new fur tippets for
Christmas.

Yrs. aff.
3rd. (Miss) F. Bunny.
XXX

Dear master
John,
I have not
learned to rite
propperly.

Love from
4th Miss F. Bunny

XXXXX
5th Miss F. Bunny

XXX

with his love,
from the 6th Master F. B.

Now Benjamin Bunny is all grown up and a father himself, do you think he is any wiser? Sadly, it seems not. Despite his frightening encounter as a young bunny, he now visits the McGregor's rubbish heap – taking his six children as well!

Benjamin should know that any rabbit (especially a parent) must always be on the look out for danger. But so stuffed with lettuces were he and his family that they fell fast asleep! No wonder Mr. McGregor found it easy to capture the Flopsy Bunnies in a sack. Were it not for the quick thinking of a clever little mouse, those young bunnies would not be alive today. At least Benjamin has learned that it is good to have helpful friends!

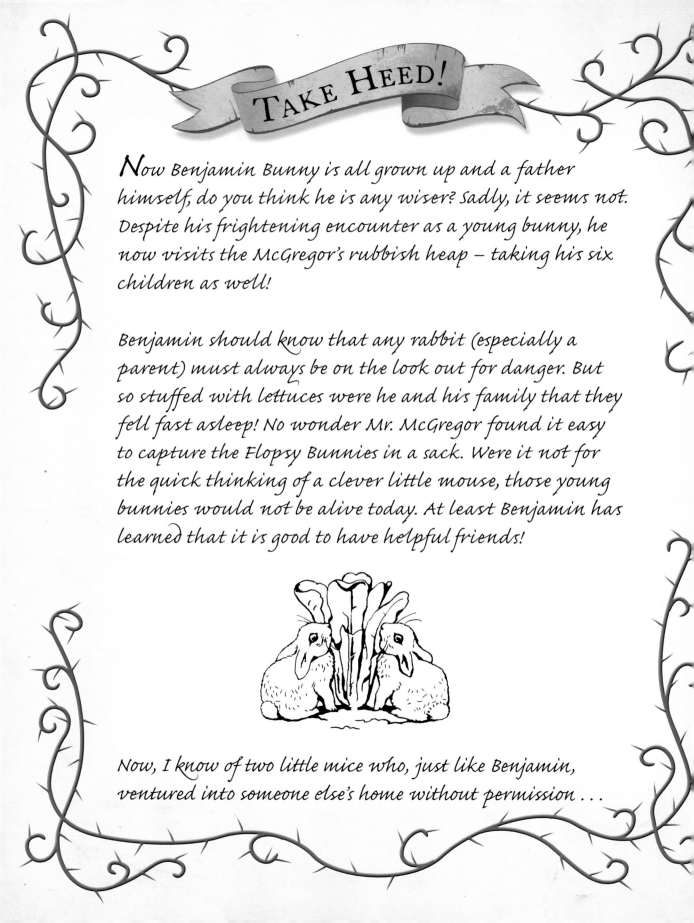

Now, I know of two little mice who, just like Benjamin, ventured into someone else's home without permission . . .

THE TALE OF
TWO BAD MICE
or

Disaster at the Doll's House

ABOUT THIS BOOK

The Tale of Two Bad Mice was written at a particularly happy time for Beatrix Potter: she and her editor, Norman Warne, were becoming firm friends, and Beatrix was sometimes included in Warne family celebrations. Norman made a new cage for Beatrix's pet mice, Tom Thumb and Hunca Munca, so that she could more easily draw them for her new book. He had also made a doll's house for his favourite niece, Winifred, and Beatrix was invited to visit and sketch this too. However, her mother objected, and so Beatrix had to make do with photographs and examples of doll's furniture and food that Norman sent her. She kept some of the furniture all her life, and it can still be seen at Hill Top, her first Lakeland home.

Beatrix dedicated the book to Winifred: "For W.M.L.W., the little girl who had the doll's house."

ONCE UPON A TIME there was a very beautiful doll's-house; it was red brick with white windows, and it had real muslin curtains and a front door and a chimney.

It belonged to two Dolls called Lucinda and Jane; at least it belonged to Lucinda, but she never ordered meals.

Jane was the Cook; but she never did any cooking, because the dinner had been bought ready-made, in a box full of shavings.

There were two red lobsters and a ham, a fish, a pudding, and some pears and oranges.

They would not come off the plates, but they were extremely beautiful.

One morning Lucinda and Jane had gone out for a drive in the doll's perambulator. There was no one in the nursery, and it was very quiet. Presently there was a little scuffling, scratching noise in a corner near the fire-place, where there was a hole under the skirting-board.

Tom Thumb put out his head for a moment, and then popped it in again.

Tom Thumb was a mouse.

A minute afterwards, Hunca Munca, his wife, put her head out, too; and when she saw that there was no one in the nursery, she ventured out on the oilcloth under the coal-box.

The doll's-house stood at the other side of the fire-place. Tom Thumb and Hunca Munca went cautiously across the hearthrug. They pushed the front door — it was not fast.

Tom Thumb and Hunca Munca went upstairs and peeped into the dining-room. Then they squeaked with joy!

Such a lovely dinner was laid out upon the table! There were tin spoons, and lead knives and forks, and two dolly-chairs — all *so* convenient!

Tom Thumb set to work at once to carve the ham. It was a beautiful shiny yellow, streaked with red.

The knife crumpled up and hurt him; he put his finger in his mouth.

"It is not boiled enough; it is hard. You have a try, Hunca Munca."

Hunca Munca stood up
in her chair, and chopped
at the ham with another
lead knife.

"It's as hard as the hams
at the cheesemonger's,"
said Hunca Munca.

The ham broke off the
plate with a jerk, and rolled
under the table.

"Let it alone," said Tom
Thumb; "give me some
fish, Hunca Munca!"

Hunca Munca tried every tin spoon in turn; the fish was glued
to the dish.

Then Tom Thumb lost his temper. He put the ham in the
middle of the floor, and hit it with the tongs and with the shovel —
bang, bang, smash, smash!

The ham flew all into pieces, for underneath the shiny paint
it was made of nothing but plaster!

Then there was no end to the rage and disappointment of Tom Thumb and Hunca Munca. They broke up the pudding, the lobsters, the pears and the oranges.

As the fish would not come off the plate, they put it into the red-hot crinkly paper fire in the kitchen; but it would not burn either.

Tom Thumb went up the kitchen chimney and looked out at the top — there was no soot.

While Tom Thumb was up the chimney, Hunca Munca had another disappointment. She found some tiny canisters upon the dresser, labelled — Rice — Coffee — Sago — but when she turned them upside down, there was nothing inside except red and blue beads.

Then those mice set to work to do all the mischief they could — especially Tom Thumb! He took Jane's clothes out of the chest of drawers in her bedroom, and he threw them out of the top floor window.

But Hunca Munca had a
frugal mind. After pulling
half the feathers out of
Lucinda's bolster, she
remembered that she herself
was in want of a feather bed.

With Tom Thumb's
assistance she carried the
bolster downstairs, and across
the hearthrug. It was difficult
to squeeze the bolster into
the mouse-hole; but they
managed it somehow.

Then Hunca Munca went back and fetched a chair,
a book-case, a bird-cage, and several small odds and ends.
The book-case and the bird-cage refused to go into
the mouse-hole.

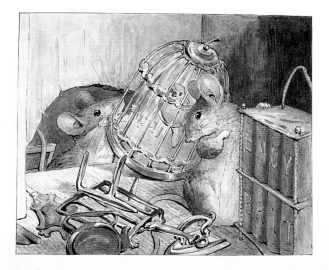

Hunca Munca left them behind the coal-box, and went to fetch a cradle.

Hunca Munca was just returning with another chair, when suddenly there was a noise of talking outside upon the landing. The mice rushed back to their hole, and the dolls came into the nursery.

What a sight met the eyes of Jane and Lucinda!

Lucinda sat upon the upset kitchen stove and stared; and Jane leant against the kitchen dresser and smiled — but neither of them made any remark.

The book-case and the bird-cage were rescued from under the coal-box — but Hunca Munca has got the cradle, and some of Lucinda's clothes.

She also has some useful pots and pans, and several other things.

The little girl that the doll's-house belonged to, said — "I will get a doll dressed like a policeman!"

But the nurse said — "I will set a mouse-trap!"

So that is the story of the two Bad Mice, — but they were not so very very naughty after all, because Tom Thumb paid for everything he broke.

He found a crooked sixpence under the hearthrug; and upon Christmas Eve, he and Hunca Munca stuffed it into one of the stockings of Lucinda and Jane.

And very early every morning — before anybody is awake — Hunca Munca comes with her dust-pan and her broom to sweep the Dollies' house!

The End . . .

. . . of the story, and, it seems, the naughtiness too!

The two little mice have learned their lesson.

Miss Lucinda Doll,
Doll's House.

Honoured Madam,
    I am sorry to hear that my wife forgot
to dust the mantelpiece, I have whipped
her. Me & my wife would be very grateful for
another kettle, the last one is full of holes.
Me & my wife do not think that it was made
of tin at all. We have nine of a family at
present & they require hot water.
    I remain honoured madam,

Yr. obedient servant,
    Thomas Thumb

Goodness me! Hunca Munca and Tom Thumb were so terribly naughty that I don't know where to begin. To start with, it was extremely rude of the two mice to sneak into the doll's house while the owners were out. And fancy destroying Jane and Lucinda's lovely dinner in such a rage! Then throwing the clothes out of the window! What an awful shock those poor dolls must have had when they returned home . . .

Still, we should remember that the mischievous mice did try to make up for their bad behaviour. And now that Hunca Munca secretly sweeps up, Jane and Lucinda have a lovely clean house to wake up to every morning.

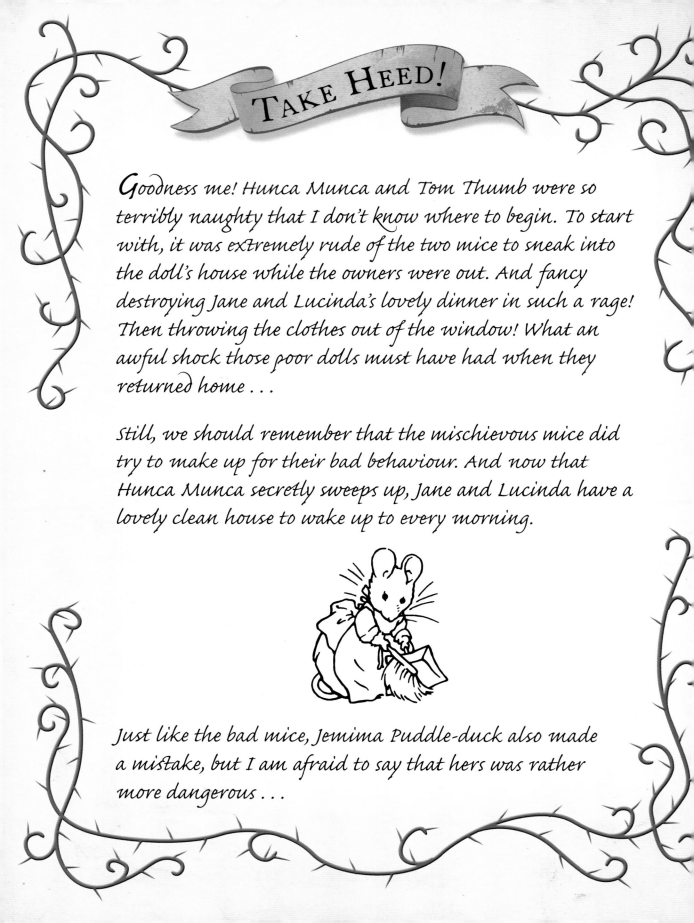

Just like the bad mice, Jemima Puddle-duck also made a mistake, but I am afraid to say that hers was rather more dangerous . . .

THE TALE OF
JEMIMA
PUDDLE-DUCK

or

The Dim-witted Duck

ABOUT THIS BOOK

Beatrix Potter's love of Hill Top and farming shine through this story. She painted her farm manager's wife, Mrs. Cannon, feeding the poultry, while the children Ralph and Betsy (to whom this "farmyard tale" is dedicated) are also illustrated. Kep the collie was Beatrix's favorite sheepdog, and Jemima herself was a real duck who lived at Hill Top. She is a most popular character: self-important, naive, but very endearing.

The story also contains many delightful views of Sawrey: Jemima's wood can still be seen, the view from the hills above the farm, across Esthwaite Water, has not changed, and the Tower Bank Arms is still the local village pub. This blend of fantasy and reality, so often to be found in Beatrix Potter's work, gives a ring of truth to her imaginary world.

WHAT A FUNNY SIGHT it is to see a brood of ducklings with a hen! — Listen to the story of Jemima Puddle-duck, who was annoyed because the farmer's wife would not let her hatch her own eggs.

Her sister-in-law, Mrs. Rebeccah Puddle-duck, was perfectly willing to leave the hatching to some one else — "I have not the patience to sit on a nest for twenty-eight days; and no more have you, Jemima. You would let them go cold; you know you would!"

"I wish to hatch my own eggs; I will hatch them all by myself," quacked Jemima Puddle-duck.

She tried to hide her eggs; but they were always found and carried off.

Jemima Puddle-duck became quite desperate. She determined to make a nest right away from the farm.

She set off on a fine spring afternoon along the cart-road that leads over the hill.

She was wearing a shawl and a poke bonnet.

When she reached the top of the hill, she saw a wood in the distance.

She thought that it looked a safe quiet spot.

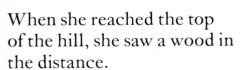

Jemima Puddle-duck was not much in the habit of flying. She ran downhill a few yards flapping her shawl, and then she jumped off into the air.

She flew beautifully when she had got a good start.

She skimmed along over the tree-tops until she saw an open place in the middle of the wood, where the trees and brushwood had been cleared.

Jemima alighted rather heavily, and began to waddle about in search of a convenient dry nesting-place.

She rather fancied a tree-stump amongst some tall fox-gloves.

But — seated upon the stump, she was startled to find an elegantly dressed gentleman reading a newspaper.

He had black prick ears and sandy-coloured whiskers.

"Quack?" said Jemima Puddle-duck, with her head and her bonnet on one side — "Quack?"

The gentleman raised his eyes above his newspaper and looked curiously at Jemima —

"Madam, have you lost your way?" said he. He had a long bushy tail which he was sitting upon, as the stump was somewhat damp.

Jemima thought him mighty civil and handsome. She explained that she had not lost her way, but that she was trying to find a convenient dry nesting-place.

"Ah! is that so? indeed!" said the gentleman with sandy whiskers, looking curiously at Jemima. He folded up the newspaper, and put it in his coat-tail pocket.

Jemima complained of the superfluous hen.

"Indeed? how interesting!

"I wish I could meet with that fowl. I would teach it to mind its own business!

"But as to a nest — there is no difficulty: I have a sackful of feathers in my wood-shed. No, my dear madam, you will be in nobody's way. You may sit there as long as you like," said the bushy long-tailed gentleman.

He led the way to a very retired, dismal-looking house amongst the fox-gloves.

It was built of faggots and turf, and there were two broken pails, one on top of another, by way of a chimney.

"This is my summer residence; you would not find my earth — my winter house — so convenient," said the hospitable gentleman.

There was a tumble-down shed at the back of the house, made of old soap-boxes. The gentleman opened the door, and showed Jemima in.

The shed was almost quite full of feathers — it was almost suffocating; but it was comfortable and very soft.

Jemima Puddle-duck was rather surprised to find such a vast quantity of feathers. But it was very comfortable; and she made a nest without any trouble at all.

When she came out, the sandy-whiskered gentleman was sitting on a log reading the newspaper — at least he had it spread out, but he was looking over the top of it.

He was so polite, that he seemed almost sorry to let Jemima go home for the night. He promised to take great care of her nest until she came back again next day.

He said he loved eggs and ducklings; he should be proud to see a fine nestful in his wood-shed. Jemima Puddle-duck came every afternoon; she laid nine eggs in the nest. They were greeny white and very large. The foxy gentleman admired them immensely. He used to turn them over and count them when Jemima was not there.

At last Jemima told him that
she intended to begin to sit
next day — "and I will bring a
bag of corn with me, so that I
need never leave my nest until
the eggs are hatched. They
might catch cold," said the
conscientious Jemima.

"Madam, I beg you not to
trouble yourself with a bag; I
will provide oats. But before you
commence your tedious sitting, I intend to give you a treat. Let us
have a dinner-party all to ourselves!
May I ask you to bring up some
herbs from the farm-garden to
make a savoury omelette? Sage and
thyme, and mint and two onions,
and some parsley. I will provide

lard for the stuff — lard for the
omelette," said the hospitable
gentleman with sandy whiskers.

Jemima Puddle-duck was a
simpleton: not even the mention
of sage and onions made her
suspicious. She went round the farm-garden, nibbling off snippets of
all the different sorts of herbs that are used for stuffing roast duck.

And she waddled into the kitchen, and got two onions out of a basket.

The collie-dog Kep met her coming out. "What are you doing with those onions? Where do you go every afternoon by yourself, Jemima Puddle-duck?"

Jemima was rather in awe of the collie; she told him the whole story.

The collie listened, with his wise head on one side; he grinned when she described the polite gentleman with sandy whiskers. He asked several questions about the wood, and about the exact position of the house and shed.

Then he went out, and trotted down the village. He went to look for two fox-hound puppies who were out at walk with the butcher.

Jemima Puddle-duck went
up the cart-road for the last
time, on a sunny afternoon.
She was rather burdened
with bunches of herbs and
two onions in a bag.

She flew over the wood, and alighted opposite the house of the
bushy long-tailed gentleman.

He was sitting on a log; he sniffed the air, and kept glancing
uneasily round the wood. When Jemima alighted he quite jumped.

"Come into the house
as soon as you have looked
at your eggs. Give me the
herbs for the omelette.
Be sharp!"

He was rather abrupt.
Jemima Puddle-duck had
never heard him speak
like that.

She felt surprised, and
uncomfortable.

While she was inside she heard pattering feet round the back of the shed. Some one with a black nose sniffed at the bottom of the door, and then locked it.

Jemima became much alarmed.

A moment afterwards there were most awful noises — barking, baying, growls and howls, squealing and groans.

And nothing more was ever seen of that foxy-whiskered gentleman.

Presently Kep opened the door of the shed, and let out Jemima Puddle-duck.

Unfortunately the puppies rushed in and gobbled up all the eggs before he could stop them.

He had a bite on his ear and both the puppies were limping.
Jemima Puddle-duck was escorted home in tears on account
of those eggs.

She laid some more in June, and she was permitted to keep them herself; but only four of them hatched.

Jemima Puddle-duck said that it was because of her nerves; but she had always been a bad sitter.

What a lucky escape!

It seems as though Jemima isn't
the only dim-witted Puddle-duck ...

The Puddle-duck Family, Farm Yard.

SALLY HENNY PENNY
AT HOME
AT THE BARN DOOR
DEC. 24TH

INDIAN CORN AND DANCING

Mr. Drake Puddle-duck, Mrs. Jemima
& Mrs. Rebeccah   R.S.V.P.

Miss Sally Henny Penny,
Barn Door.

Mr. Drake Puddle-duck and Mrs. Jemima
accept with much pleasure, but Mrs.
Rebeccah is laid up with a sore throat.

Mrs. Ribstone Pippin,
Lakefield Cottage.

Dear Mrs. Ribby,
Can you lend me a red flannel
petticoat to wear as a comforter.
I have laid up with a sort throat
and I do not wish to call in Dr.
Maggotty. It is 12 inches long, a
mustard leaf is no use.

Yr. sincere friend,
Rebeccah puddleduck.

Mrs. Rebeccah Puddleduck,
Farm Yard.

Dear Beccy,
I am sorry to hear of your sore throat, but what can you expect if you will stand on your head in a pond? I will bring the flannel petticoat & some more head drops directly.

Yr. sincere friend,
Ribby.

TAKE HEED!

Jemima Puddle-duck must surely be the luckiest duck in the world! Despite her trusting ways, she escaped the clutches of a cunning fox (though not without the help of a wise collie dog). But, I am sorry to say that I also believe Jemima to be one of the world's most foolish birds. It seems the dim-witted duck had not the slightest idea that the handsome stranger was, in fact, a fox – her deadliest enemy!

Let's hope she is never taken in by appearances again. Especially by smooth, well-dressed gentlemen who ask her to collect herbs for a duck stuffing! Perhaps if Jemima stops and thinks a little more, things will turn out better in the future?

Unfortunately, when Jemima later meets a cat, young Tom Kitten, you will see that her common sense is not much improved!

THE TALE OF
TOM KITTEN

or

Beware of Dilly-dallying Ducks

ABOUT THIS BOOK

By the time Beatrix Potter started writing *The Tale of Tom Kitten*, she had owned Hill Top farm, in the Lake District village of Sawrey, for a year. The expansion of the farmhouse was finished, and Beatrix was enthusiastically planning her cottage garden. She could not completely desert her property for writing, and both house and garden feature in the story. Mrs. Tabitha Twitchit leads her children up the path to Hill Top's front door, while inside we see its staircase and bedrooms. The kittens romp through the garden's flowers to jump up on the wall overlooking Sawrey, and the ducks march across the farmyard.

    Beatrix used the same kitten as a model for both Miss Moppet and Tom. "It is very young and pretty and a most fearful pickle." She dedicated this story to "all Pickles – especially to those that get upon my garden wall".

ONCE UPON A TIME
there were three little
kittens, and their names
were — Mittens, Tom Kitten,
and Moppet.

They had dear little fur
coats of their own; and they
tumbled about the doorstep
and played in the dust.

But one day their mother —
Mrs. Tabitha Twitchit —
expected friends to tea;
so she fetched the kittens
indoors, to wash and
dress them, before the
fine company arrived.

First she scrubbed their faces
(this one is Moppet).

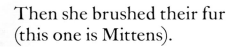

Then she brushed their fur
(this one is Mittens).

Then she combed their
tails and whiskers (this is
Tom Kitten).

Tom was very naughty,
and he scratched.

Mrs. Tabitha dressed
Moppet and Mittens
in clean pinafores and
tuckers; and then she
took all sorts of elegant
uncomfortable clothes
out of a chest of drawers,
in order to dress up her
son Thomas.

Tom Kitten was very fat, and
he had grown; several buttons
burst off. His mother sewed
them on again.

When the three kittens were
ready, Mrs. Tabitha unwisely
turned them out into the garden,
to be out of the way while she
made hot buttered toast.

"Now keep your frocks clean,
children! You must walk on
your hind legs.

"Keep away from the dirty ash-pit, and from Sally Henny-penny, and from the pig-stye and the Puddle-ducks."

Moppet and Mittens walked down the garden path unsteadily. Presently they trod upon their pinafores and fell on their noses. When they stood up there were several green smears!

"Let us climb up the rockery, and sit on the garden wall," said Moppet.

They turned their pinafores back to front, and went up with a skip and a jump; Moppet's white tucker fell down into the road.

Tom Kitten was quite unable to jump when walking upon his hind legs in trousers. He came up the rockery by degrees, breaking the ferns, and shedding buttons right and left.

He was all in pieces when he reached the top of the wall.

Moppet and Mittens tried to pull him together; his hat fell off, and the rest of his buttons burst.

While they were in difficulties, there was a pit pat paddle pat! and the three Puddle-ducks came along the hard high road, marching one behind the other and doing the goose step — pit pat paddle pat! pit pat waddle pat!

They stopped and stood in a row, and stared up at the kittens. They had very small eyes and looked surprised.

Then the two duck-birds, Rebeccah and Jemima Puddle-duck, picked up the hat and tucker and put them on.

Mittens laughed so that she fell off the wall. Moppet and Tom descended after her; the pinafores and all the rest of Tom's clothes came off on the way down.

"Come! Mr. Drake Puddle-duck," said Moppet — "Come and help us to dress him! Come and button up Tom!"

Mr. Drake Puddle-duck advanced in a slow sideways manner, and picked up the various articles.

But he put them on *himself!* They fitted him even worse than Tom Kitten.

"It's a very fine morning!" said Mr. Drake Puddle-duck.

And he and Jemima and Rebeccah Puddle-duck set off up the road, keeping step — pit pat, paddle pat! pit pat, waddle pat!

Then Tabitha Twitchit came down the garden and found her kittens on the wall with no clothes on.

She pulled them off the wall, smacked them, and took them back to the house.

"My friends will arrive in a minute, and you are not fit to be seen; I am affronted," said Mrs. Tabitha Twitchit.

She sent them upstairs; and I am sorry to say she told her friends that they were in bed with the measles; which was not true.

Quite the contrary; they were not in bed; *not* in the least.

Somehow there were very extraordinary noises over-head, which disturbed the dignity and repose of the tea-party.

And I think that some day I shall have to make another, larger, book, to tell you more about Tom Kitten!

As for the Puddle-ducks — they went into a pond.

The clothes all came off directly, because there were no buttons.

And Mr. Drake Puddle-duck, and Jemima and Rebeccah, have been looking for them ever since.

The End.

It seems that Puddle-ducks and kittens together cause no end of trouble. And Tom Kitten needs no encouragement to be naughty at all!

To Francisca Burn

August 1912

My dear "Double Dutch"
This is a letter from Tom Kitten. I am a bad cat; has your dolly told you what I did when you were upstairs in Miss Potter's room?

I shook hands with Dolly very - very - hard --- and her hand comed off!

After you went away Miss Potter saw a funny little thing lying in the middle of the hall, on the matting. She could not think what it was, and when she picked I up, it was a hand! I am now nearly grown up now. The big cat Fluffy is teaching me to catch mice.

Tibby our old cat has caught some rats in the barn. They are stealing the corn, and nibbling the potatoes.

Now good bye from

Tom Kitten

When Tom and his brothers and sisters were told to keep their best clothes clean, the last thing their mother expected was for them to return to the house with nothing on at all! They were smacked and sent upstairs, but then caused mayhem in their bedroom. Those naughty kittens! However, perhaps we should not be too hard on the little mischief makers. After all, kittens will be kittens – they love to play and make a mess. Let's hope they become more sensible as they grow older!

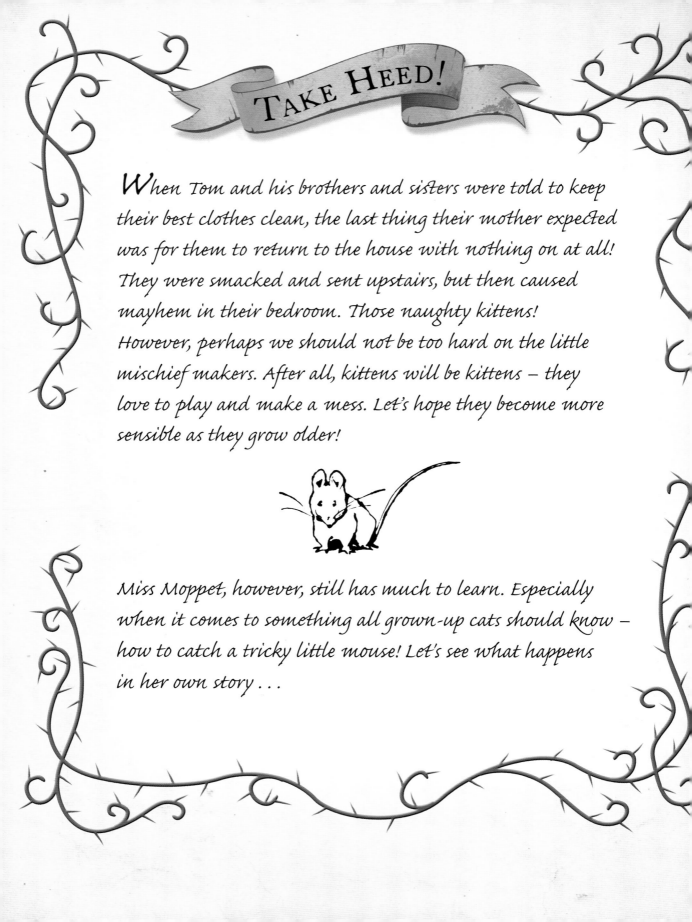

Miss Moppet, however, still has much to learn. Especially when it comes to something all grown-up cats should know – how to catch a tricky little mouse! Let's see what happens in her own story . . .

THE STORY OF
MISS MOPPET

or

Being Small is No Excuse

ABOUT THIS BOOK

The Story of Miss Moppet was the second book to be published as a fold-out concertina (alongside *The Story of A Fierce Bad Rabbit*), in time for Christmas 1906. Moppet is Tom Kitten's sister, and the simple story about her exploits with a cheeky mouse is intended for very young children. Beatrix Potter did not want to upset her young audience unduly, writing on the draft for one picture, "She should catch him by the tail – less unpleasant." All ends happily in this delightful story, however.

The book was reprinted in a standard format in 1916 to please the bookshops, and listed at the end of the series of Peter Rabbit books with the other three titles for very young children, *The Story of A Fierce Bad Rabbit*, and *Appley Dapply's* and *Cecily Parsley's Nursery Rhymes*.

THIS IS A PUSSY called Miss Moppet, she thinks she has heard a mouse!

This is the Mouse peeping out behind the cupboard, and making fun of Miss Moppet. He is not afraid of a kitten.

This is Miss Moppet jumping just too late; she misses the Mouse and hits her own head.

She thinks it is a very
hard cupboard!

The Mouse watches
Miss Moppet from the
top of the cupboard.

Miss Moppet ties up her
head in a duster, and sits
before the fire.
  The Mouse thinks she is
looking very ill. He comes
sliding down the bell-pull.

Miss Moppet looks worse and worse. The Mouse comes a little nearer.

Miss Moppet holds her poor head in her paws, and looks at him through a hole in the duster. The Mouse comes *very* close.

And then all of a sudden — Miss Moppet jumps upon the Mouse!

And because the Mouse has teased Miss Moppet — Miss Moppet thinks she will tease the Mouse; which is not at all nice of Miss Moppet.

She ties him up in the duster, and tosses it about like a ball.

But she forgot about that hole in the duster; and when she untied it — there was no Mouse!

He has wriggled out and run away; and he is dancing a jig on the top of the cupboard!

The End . . .
but not for the plucky mouse who lived to tell the tale!

And here is further evidence of
Miss Moppet's mischievous behaviour.

(Private) Master Tom Kitten, Hill Top Farm

SALLY HENNY PENNY

at HOME

AT THE BARN DOOR

DEC. 24TH

INDIAN CORN AND DANCING

Master T. Kitten, Miss Moppet
& Miss Mittens Kitten.   R.S.V.P.

Miss Sally henny penny,
Barn Door.

Dear henny,
Me and Moppet and Mittens will
all come, if our Ma doesn't
catch us.

T. Kitten.

Tom Kitten and Miss Moppet are brother and sister and they certainly have something in common – mischievousness!

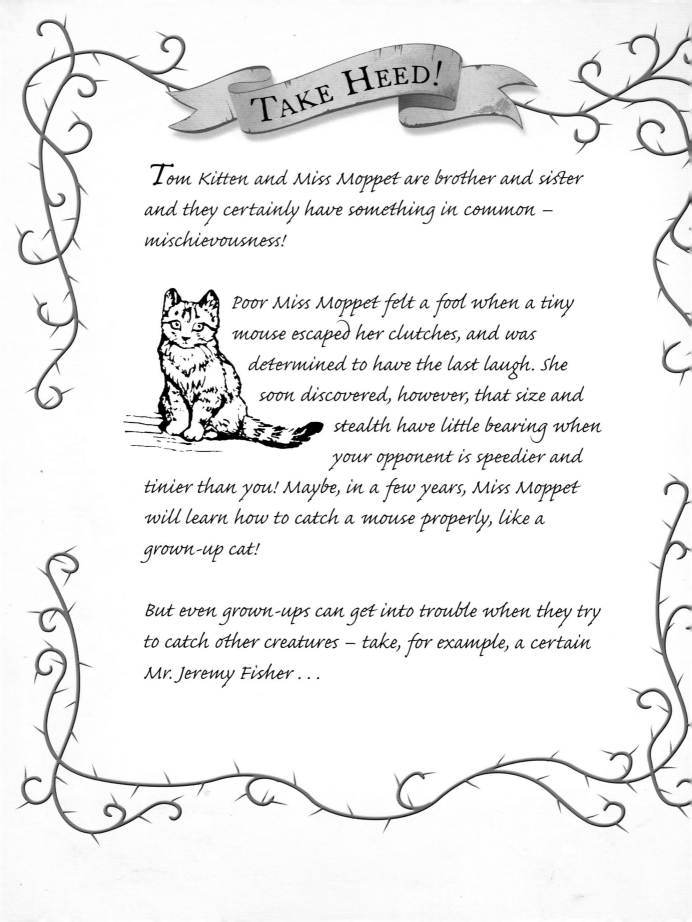

Poor Miss Moppet felt a fool when a tiny mouse escaped her clutches, and was determined to have the last laugh. She soon discovered, however, that size and stealth have little bearing when your opponent is speedier and tinier than you! Maybe, in a few years, Miss Moppet will learn how to catch a mouse properly, like a grown-up cat!

But even grown-ups can get into trouble when they try to catch other creatures – take, for example, a certain Mr. Jeremy Fisher . . .

THE TALE OF
MR. JEREMY FISHER

or

The Treacherous Trout

ABOUT THIS BOOK

Mr. Jeremy Fisher had existed in Beatrix Potter's imagination for many years before his story was eventually published in 1906. He first appeared in 1893 in a picture letter to Eric Moore, written by Beatrix the day after she had sent the Peter Rabbit story to his brother Noel. In 1894, she produced a series of black-and-white frog drawings which were published in a children's annual and in 1902, Beatrix discussed Mr. Jeremy with her editor, Norman Warne. After Norman's death in 1905, Beatrix needed to work and took up the story with Harold, Norman's brother, as her new editor. "I feel as if my work and your kindness will be my greatest comfort." Perhaps the solitary hours spent sketching tranquil scenes in the Lake District did bring Beatrix comfort: the book certainly contains some of her most beautiful paintings. It is dedicated to Stephanie Hyde Parker, "from Cousin B".

ONCE UPON A TIME there was a frog called Mr. Jeremy Fisher; he lived in a little damp house amongst the buttercups at the edge of a pond.

The water was all slippy-sloppy in the larder and in the back passage.

But Mr. Jeremy liked getting his feet wet; nobody ever scolded him, and he never caught a cold!

He was quite pleased when he looked out and saw large drops of rain, splashing in the pond —

"I will get some worms and go
fishing and catch a dish of minnows
for my dinner," said Mr. Jeremy
Fisher. "If I catch more than
five fish, I will invite my friends
Mr. Alderman Ptolemy Tortoise
and Sir Isaac Newton. The
Alderman, however, eats salad."

Mr. Jeremy put on a macintosh,
and a pair of shiny goloshes;

he took his rod and basket, and
set off with enormous hops to
the place where he kept his boat.
   The boat was round and green,
and very like the other lily-leaves.
It was tied to a water-plant in the
middle of the pond.

Mr. Jeremy took a reed pole, and
pushed the boat out into open
water. "I know a good place for
minnows," said Mr. Jeremy Fisher.

Mr. Jeremy stuck his pole into
the mud and fastened the boat to it.

Then he settled himself cross-
legged and arranged his fishing
tackle.

He had the dearest little red
float. His rod was a tough stalk
of grass, his line was a fine
long white horse-hair,

and he tied a little wriggling
worm at the end.

The rain trickled down his
back, and for nearly an hour
he stared at the float.

"This is getting tiresome,
I think I should like some
lunch," said Mr. Jeremy Fisher.

He punted back again amongst the water-plants, and took some lunch out of his basket.

"I will eat a butterfly sandwich, and wait till the shower is over," said Mr. Jeremy Fisher.

A great big water-beetle came up underneath the lily-leaf and tweaked the toe of one of his goloshes.

Mr. Jeremy crossed his legs up shorter, out of reach, and went on eating his sandwich.

Once or twice something moved about with a rustle and a splash amongst the rushes at the side of the pond.

"I trust that is not a rat," said Mr. Jeremy Fisher; "I think I had better get away from here."

Mr. Jeremy shoved the boat out again a little way, and dropped in the bait. There was a bite almost directly; the float gave a tremendous bobbit!

"A minnow! a minnow! I have him by the nose!" cried Mr. Jeremy Fisher, jerking up his rod.

But what a horrible surprise! Instead of a smooth fat minnow, Mr. Jeremy landed little Jack Sharp the stickleback, covered with spines!

The stickleback floundered about the boat, pricking and snapping until he was quite out of breath.

Then he jumped back into the water.

And a shoal of other little fishes put their heads out, and laughed at Mr. Jeremy Fisher.

And while Mr. Jeremy sat disconsolately on the edge of his boat —

— sucking his sore fingers and peering down into the water — a *much* worse thing happened; a really *frightful* thing it would have been, if Mr. Jeremy had not been wearing a macintosh!

A great big enormous trout came up — ker-pflop-p-p-p! with a splash —

— and it seized Mr. Jeremy with a snap, "Ow! Ow! Ow!" — and then it turned and dived down to the bottom of the pond!

But the trout was so displeased with the taste of the macintosh, that in less than half a minute it spat him out again; and the only thing it swallowed was Mr. Jeremy's goloshes.

Mr. Jeremy bounced up to the surface of the water, like a cork and the bubbles out of a soda water bottle; and he swam with all his might to the edge of the pond.

He scrambled out on the first bank he came to, and he hopped home across the meadow with his macintosh all in tatters.

"What a mercy that was not a pike!" said Mr. Jeremy Fisher.

"I have lost my rod and basket; but it does not much matter, for I am sure I should never have dared to go fishing again!"

He put some sticking plaster on his fingers, and his friends both came to dinner. He could not offer them fish, but he had something else in his larder.

Sir Isaac Newton wore his black and gold waistcoat.

And Mr. Alderman Ptolemy Tortoise brought a salad with him in a string bag.

And instead of a nice dish of minnows — they had a roasted grass-hopper with ladybird sauce; which frogs consider a beautiful treat; but I think it must have been nasty!

The End . . .

of this particular story.

However, it seems that Mr. Jeremy Fisher's bachelor status has become the subject of considerable gossip . . .

Master D. Fayle,
Kylimore.

Dear Master Drew,
I hear that you think that there ought to be a 'Mrs. J. Fisher'. Our friend is at present taking mud baths at the bottom of the pond, which may be the reason why your letter has not been answered quick by return. I will do my best to advise him, but I fear he remembers the sad fate of his elder brother who disobeyed his mother, and he was gobbled up by a lily white duck! If my friend Jeremy Fisher gets married, I will certainly tell you, & send a bit of wedding cake. One of our friends is going into the next book. He is fatter than Jeremy; and he has shorter legs.

Yrs. with compliments,
Sir Isacc Newton.

Master Drew Fayle,
Kytimore.

Dear Master Drew,
I hear that you are interested in the
domestic arrangements of our friend
Jeremy Fisher. I am of opinion that
his dinner parties would be much more
agreeable if there were a lady to preside
at the table. I do not care for roast
grasshoppers. His housekeeping and cookery
do not come up to the standard to which I
am accustomed at the Mansion House.

Yrs. truly,
Alderman Pt. Tortoise.

Master D. Fayle,
Kylimore,
Co. Dublin.

Dear Master Drew,
In answer to your very kind inquiry, I live
alone; I am not married. When I bought my
sprigged waistcoat & my maroon tail-coat,
I had hopes... But I am alone... If there
were a "Mrs. Jeremy Fisher" she might object
to snails. It is some satisfaction to be able to
have as much water & mud in the house
as a person likes.
Thanking you for your touching inquiry,

Yr. devoted friend,
Jeremiah Fisher.

Master Drew Fayle,
Kylimore, Co. Dublin.

Dear Master Drew,
If you please Sir I am a widow; and I
think it is very wrong that there is not any
Mrs. Jeremy Fisher, but I would not marry
Mr. Jeremy not for worlds, the way he does
live in that house all slippy-sloppy; not any
lady would stand it, and not a bit of good
starching his cravats.

Yr. obedient washerwoman,
Tiggy Winkle.

*W*hat a lucky escape Mr. Jeremy Fisher had! Snapped up by a large trout, it would only have taken one GULP and that would have been the end of the unfortunate frog! (Thank goodness the fish disliked the taste of Mr. Jeremy's mackintosh.) If there's one thing we can learn from this tale, it's that life is full of surprises. And Mr. Jeremy certainly knows that he should expect the unexpected from now on!

Despite his terrible shock, Mr. Jeremy recovered himself and enjoyed a nice meal with his friends that evening. But do take care on your next fishing trip, Mr. Jeremy! Or perhaps you should stick to roasted grasshoppers for dinner in future?

Mr. Jeremy's awful experience reminds me of another little fellow, who was nearly gobbled up – not by a fish this time, but by a very large rat . . .

THE TALE OF
SAMUEL WHISKERS
OR THE ROLY-POLY PUDDING

or

*The Rat's Recipe and How to
Avoid Becoming an Ingredient:
A Practical Guide for Kittens*

ABOUT THIS BOOK

When this story was first published in 1908, it was entitled *The Roly-Poly Pudding*, and appeared in the larger size used for *The Pie and The Patty-Pan*. In 1926 it was reduced to the standard size and given the title we now know it by.

The tale was actually written in 1906, when Beatrix was exploring Hill Top, the farm she had recently bought. She described the house in a letter to a friend. "It really is delightful – if the rats could be stopped out! . . . I never saw such a place for hide and seek and funny cupboards and closets." Here was her inspiration for the further adventures of Tom Kitten: an old farmhouse, and her pet rat, to whom the book is dedicated, "In remembrance of Sammy, the intelligent pink-eyed representative of a persecuted (but irrepressible) race. An affectionate little friend and most accomplished thief."

Once upon a time there was an old cat, called Mrs. Tabitha Twitchit, who was an anxious parent. She used to lose her kittens continually, and whenever they were lost they were always in mischief!

On baking day she determined to shut them up in a cupboard.

She caught Moppet and Mittens, but she could not find Tom.

Mrs. Tabitha went up and down all over the house, mewing for Tom Kitten. She looked in the pantry under the staircase, and she searched the best spare bedroom that was all covered up with dust sheets. She went right upstairs and looked into the attics, but she could not find him anywhere.

It was an old, old house, full of cupboards and passages. Some of the walls were four feet thick, and there used to be queer noises inside them, as if there might be a little secret staircase. Certainly there were odd little jagged doorways in the wainscot, and things disappeared at night — especially cheese and bacon.

Mrs. Tabitha became more and more distracted, and mewed dreadfully.

While their mother was
searching the house,
Moppet and Mittens had
got into mischief.

The cupboard door was
not locked, so they pushed
it open and came out.

They went straight to the dough which was set to rise in a pan before the fire.

They patted it with their little soft paws — "Shall we make dear little muffins?" said Mittens to Moppet.

But just at that moment somebody knocked at the front door, and Moppet jumped into the flour barrel in a fright.

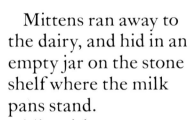

Mittens ran away to the dairy, and hid in an empty jar on the stone shelf where the milk pans stand.

The visitor was a neighbour, Mrs. Ribby; she had called to borrow some yeast.

Mrs. Tabitha came downstairs mewing dreadfully — "Come in, Cousin Ribby, come in, and sit ye down! I'm in sad trouble, Cousin Ribby," said Tabitha, shedding tears. "I've lost my dear son Thomas; I'm afraid the rats have got him." She wiped her eyes with her apron.

"He's a bad kitten, Cousin Tabitha; he made a cat's cradle of my best bonnet last time I came to tea. Where have you looked for him?"

"All over the house!
The rats are too many for
me. What a thing it is to
have an unruly family!"
said Mrs. Tabitha Twitchit.

"I'm not afraid of rats;
I will help you to find him;
and whip him too! What is
all that soot in the fender?"

"The chimney wants sweeping — Oh, dear me, Cousin Ribby — now Moppet and Mittens are gone!

"They have both got out of the cupboard!"

Ribby and Tabitha set to work to search the house thoroughly again. They poked under the beds with Ribby's umbrella, and they rummaged in cupboards. They even fetched a candle, and looked inside a

clothes chest in one of the attics. They could not find anything, but once they heard a door bang and somebody scuttered downstairs.

"Yes, it is infested with rats," said Tabitha tearfully. "I caught seven young ones out of one hole in the back kitchen, and we had them for dinner last Saturday. And once I saw the old father rat — an enormous old rat, Cousin Ribby. I was just going to jump upon him, when he showed his yellow teeth at me and whisked down the hole.

"The rats get upon my nerves, Cousin Ribby," said Tabitha.

Ribby and Tabitha searched and searched. They both heard a curious roly-poly noise under the attic floor. But there was nothing to be seen.

They returned to the kitchen. "Here's one of your kittens at least," said Ribby, dragging Moppet out of the flour barrel.

They shook the flour off her and set her down on the kitchen floor. She seemed to be in a terrible fright.

"Oh! Mother, Mother," said Moppet, "there's been an old woman rat in the kitchen, and she's stolen some of the dough!"

The two cats ran to look at the dough pan. Sure enough there were marks of little scratching fingers, and a lump of dough was gone!

"Which way did she go, Moppet?"

But Moppet had been too much frightened to peep out of the barrel again.

Ribby and Tabitha took her with them to keep her safely in sight, while they went on with their search.

They went into the dairy.

The first thing they found was Mittens, hiding in an empty jar.

They tipped up the jar, and she scrambled out.

"Oh, Mother, Mother!" said Mittens —

"Oh! Mother, Mother, there has been an old man rat in the dairy — a dreadful 'normous big rat, Mother; and he's stolen a pat of butter and the rolling-pin."

Ribby and Tabitha looked at one another.

"A rolling-pin and butter! Oh, my poor son Thomas!" exclaimed Tabitha, wringing her paws.

"A rolling-pin?" said Ribby. "Did we not hear a roly-poly noise in the attic when we were looking into that chest?"

Ribby and Tabitha rushed upstairs again. Sure enough the roly-poly noise was still going on quite distinctly under the attic floor.

"This is serious, Cousin Tabitha," said Ribby. "We must send for John Joiner at once, with a saw."

*

Now this is what had been happening to Tom Kitten, and it shows how very unwise it is to go up a chimney in a very old house, where a person does not know his way, and where there are enormous rats.

Tom Kitten did not want to be shut up in a cupboard. When he saw that his mother was going to bake, he determined to hide.

He looked about for a nice convenient place, and he fixed upon the chimney.

The fire had only just been lighted, and it was not hot; but there was a white choky smoke from the green sticks. Tom Kitten got upon the fender and looked up. It was a big old-fashioned fire-place.

The chimney itself was wide enough inside for a man to stand up and walk about. So there was plenty of room for a little Tom Cat.

He jumped right up into the fire-place, balancing himself upon the iron bar where the kettle hangs.

Tom Kitten took another big jump off the bar, and landed on a ledge high up inside the chimney, knocking down some soot into the fender.

Tom Kitten coughed and choked with the smoke; and he could hear the sticks beginning to crackle and burn in the fire-place down below. He made up his mind to climb right to the top, and get out on the slates, and try to catch sparrows.

"I cannot go back. If I slipped I might fall in the fire and singe my beautiful tail and my little blue jacket."

The chimney was a very big old-fashioned one. It was built in the days when people burnt logs of wood upon the hearth.

The chimney stack stood up above the roof like a little stone tower, and the daylight shone down from the top, under the slanting slates that kept out the rain.

Tom Kitten was getting very frightened! He climbed up, and up, and up.

Then he waded sideways through inches of soot. He was like a little sweep himself.

It was most confusing in the dark. One flue seemed to lead into another.

There was less smoke, but Tom Kitten felt quite lost.

He scrambled up and up; but before he reached the chimney top he came to a place where somebody had loosened a stone in the wall. There were some mutton bones lying about —

"This seems funny," said Tom Kitten. "Who has been gnawing bones up here in the chimney? I wish I had never come! And what a funny smell? It is something like mouse; only dreadfully strong. It makes me sneeze," said Tom Kitten.

He squeezed through the hole in the wall, and dragged himself along a most uncomfortably tight passage where there was scarcely any light.

He groped his way carefully for several yards; he was at the back of the skirting-board in the attic, where there is a little mark * in the picture.

All at once he fell head over heels in the dark, down a hole, and landed on a heap of very dirty rags.

When Tom Kitten picked himself up and looked about him — he found himself in a place that he had never seen before, although he had lived all his life in the house.

It was a very small stuffy fusty room, with boards, and rafters, and cobwebs, and lath and plaster. Opposite to him — as far away as he could sit — was an enormous rat.

"What do you mean by tumbling into my

bed all covered with smuts?" said the rat, chattering his teeth.

"Please, sir, the chimney wants sweeping," said poor Tom Kitten.

"Anna Maria! Anna Maria!" squeaked the rat. There was a pattering noise and an old woman rat poked her head round a rafter. All in a minute she rushed upon Tom Kitten, and before he knew what was happening —

His coat was pulled off, and he was rolled up in a bundle, and tied with string in very hard knots.

Anna Maria did the tying. The old rat watched her and took snuff. When she had finished, they both sat staring at him with their mouths open.

"Anna Maria," said the old man rat (whose name was Samuel Whiskers) — "Anna Maria, make me a kitten dumpling roly-poly pudding for my dinner."

"It requires dough and a pat of butter, and a rolling-pin," said Anna Maria, considering Tom Kitten with her head on one side.

"No," said Samuel Whiskers, "make it properly, Anna Maria, with breadcrumbs."

"Nonsense! Butter and dough," replied Anna Maria.

The two rats consulted together for a few minutes and then went away.

Samuel Whiskers got through a hole in the wainscot, and went boldly down the front staircase to the dairy to get the butter. He did not meet anybody.

He made a second journey for the rolling-pin. He pushed it in front of him with his paws, like a brewer's man trundling a barrel.

He could hear Ribby and Tabitha talking, but they were busy lighting the candle to look into the chest. They did not see him.

Anna Maria went down by way of the skirting-board and a window shutter to the kitchen to steal the dough.

She borrowed a small saucer, and scooped up the dough with her paws.

She did not observe Moppet.

While Tom Kitten was left alone under the floor of the attic, he wriggled about and tried to mew for help.

But his mouth was full of soot and cobwebs, and he was tied up in such very tight knots, he could not make anybody hear him.

Except a spider who came out of a crack in the ceiling and examined the knots critically, from a safe distance.

It was a judge of knots because it had a habit of tying up unfortunate blue-bottles. It did not offer to assist him.

Tom Kitten wriggled and squirmed until he was quite exhausted.

Presently the rats came back and set to work to make him into a dumpling. First they smeared him with butter, and then they rolled him in the dough.

"Will not the string be very indigestible, Anna Maria?" inquired Samuel Whiskers.

Anna Maria said she thought that it was of no consequence; but she wished that Tom Kitten would hold his head still, as it disarranged the pastry. She laid hold of his ears.

Tom Kitten bit and spat, and mewed and wriggled; and the rolling-pin went roly-poly, roly; roly, poly, roly. The rats each held an end.

"His tail is sticking out! You did not fetch enough dough, Anna Maria."

"I fetched as much as I could carry," replied Anna Maria.

"I do not think" — said Samuel Whiskers, pausing to take a look at Tom Kitten — "I do *not* think it will be a good pudding. It smells sooty."

Anna Maria was about to argue the

point when all at once there began to be other sounds up above — the rasping noise of a saw; and the noise of a little dog, scratching and yelping!

The rats dropped the rolling-pin, and listened attentively.

"We are discovered and interrupted, Anna Maria; let us collect our property — and other people's — and depart at once.

"I fear that we shall be obliged to leave this pudding.

"But I am persuaded that the knots would have proved indigestible, whatever you may urge to the contrary."

"Come away at once and help me to tie up some mutton bones in a counterpane," said Anna Maria. "I have got half a smoked ham hidden in the chimney."

So it happened that by the time John Joiner had got the plank up — there was nobody under the floor except the rolling-pin and Tom Kitten in a very dirty dumpling!

But there was a strong smell of rats; and John Joiner spent the rest of the morning sniffing and whining, and wagging his tail, and going round and round with his head in the hole like a gimlet.

Then he nailed the plank down again, and put his tools in his bag, and came downstairs.

The cat family had quite recovered. They invited him to stay to dinner.

The dumpling had been peeled off Tom Kitten, and made separately into a bag pudding, with currants in it to hide the smuts.

They had been obliged to put Tom Kitten into a hot bath to get the butter off.

John Joiner smelt the pudding; but he regretted that he had not time to stay to dinner, because he had just finished making a wheelbarrow for Miss Potter, and she had ordered two hen-coops.

And when I was going to the post late in the afternoon — I looked up the lane from the corner, and I saw Mr. Samuel Whiskers and his wife on the run, with big bundles on a little wheelbarrow, which looked very like mine.

They were just turning in at the gate to the barn of Farmer Potatoes.
Samuel Whiskers was puffing and out of breath. Anna Maria was
still arguing in shrill tones.

She seemed to know her way,
and she seemed to have a
quantity of luggage.

I am sure *I* never gave
her leave to borrow my
wheelbarrow!

They went into the barn,
and hauled their parcels
with a bit of string to the
top of the hay mow.

After that, there were no more rats for a long time at Tabitha Twitchit's.

As for Farmer Potatoes, he has been driven nearly distracted. There are rats, and rats, and rats in his barn! They eat up the chicken food, and steal the oats and bran, and make holes in the meal bags.

And they are all descended from Mr. and Mrs. Samuel Whiskers — children and grand-children and great great grand-children.

There is no end to them!

Moppet and Mittens have grown up into very good rat-catchers.

They go out rat-catching in the village, and they find plenty of employment. They charge so much a dozen, and earn their living very comfortably.

They hang up the rats' tails in a row on the barn door, to show how many they have caught — dozens and dozens of them.

But Tom Kitten has always been afraid of a rat; he never durst face anything that is bigger than —

A Mouse.

Will poor Tom Kitten ever recover? surely this incident will have cured him of his naughtiness!

At least Samuel Whiskers got his
comeuppance, in the end . . .

To Samuel Rat,
High Barn.

Sir,

I hereby give you one day's notice to
quit my barn & stables and byre, with your
wife, children, grand children & great grand
children to the latest generation.

signed: William Potatoes,
Farmer.

witness: Gilbert Cat & John Stoat-Ferret.

Farmer Potatoes,
The Priddings.

Sir,

I have opened a Letter
addressed to one Samuel Rat. If
Samuel Rat means me, I inform
you I shall not go, and you can't
turn us out.

Yrs. etc.

Samuel Whiskers.

Mr. Obediah Rat,
Barley Mill.

Dear Friend Obediah,
Expect us - bag and baggage - at 9 o'clock in the morning. Am sorry to come upon you suddenly; but my landlord William Potatoes has given me one days notice to quit. I am of opinion that it is not legal & I could sit till Candlemas because the notice is not addressed to my proper surname. I would stand up to William Potatoes, but my wife will not face John Stoat-Ferret, so we have decided on a midnight flitting as it is full-moon. I think there are 96 of us, but am not certain. Had it been the Mayday term we could have gone to the Field Drains, but it is out of the question at this season. Trusting that the meal bags are full.

Yr. obliged friend,
Samuel Whiskers.

Poor little Tom Kitten! He certainly got more than he bargained for when he climbed up that chimney. The mischievous kitten thought it would be fun – but, oh, how wrong he was! Imagine being rolled up in dough by an enormous rat! If it had not been for the arrival of John Joiner, I am quite sure that Tom Kitten would have been eaten up for pudding and never seen again.

I think you'll agree that climbing up a chimney is a silly thing for anyone to do – particularly a kitten in a house overrun by rats. And it is hardly surprising to find that Tom has been afraid of rats ever since.

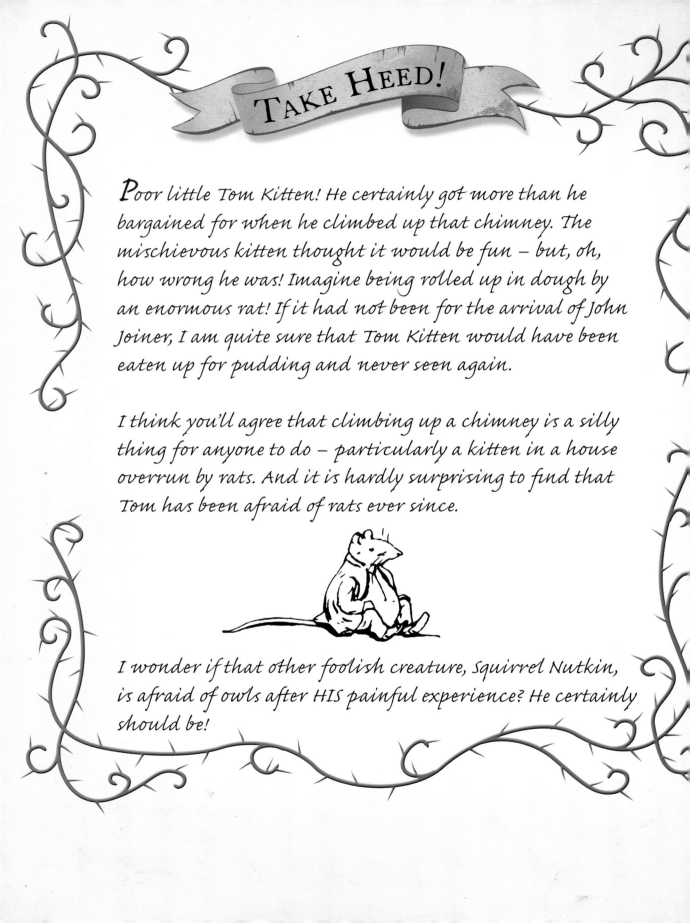

I wonder if that other foolish creature, Squirrel Nutkin, is afraid of owls after HIS painful experience? He certainly should be!

THE TALE OF
SQUIRREL NUTKIN
or
Practice Good Manners
if you Value your Tail

ABOUT THIS BOOK

In 1901, Beatrix Potter was spending the summer with her family in Lingholm, a house on the shores of Derwentwater in the Lake District. She wrote a letter all about the squirrels she saw there to eight-year-old Norah Moore, daughter of her former governess: "An old lady who lives on the island says she thinks they come over the lake when her nuts are ripe; but I wonder how they can get across the water? Perhaps they make little rafts!" The letter then goes on to relate the story of Nutkin, the cheeky squirrel who is finally punished by Old Brown, an owl whom Beatrix has substituted for the old lady of her letter.

The finished book was dedicated to Norah. It contains many views of the beautiful lake, Derwentwater, largely unchanged today.

THIS IS A TALE about a tail — a tail that belonged to a little red squirrel, and his name was Nutkin.

He had a brother called Twinkleberry, and a great many cousins; they lived in a wood at the edge of a lake.

In the middle of the lake there is an island covered with trees and nut bushes; and amongst those trees stands a hollow oak-tree, which is the house of an owl who is called Old Brown.

One autumn when the nuts were ripe, and the leaves on the hazel bushes were golden and green — Nutkin and Twinkleberry and all the other little squirrels came out of the wood, and down to the edge of the lake.

They made little rafts out of twigs, and they paddled away over the water to Owl Island to gather nuts.

Each squirrel had a little sack and a large oar, and spread out his tail for a sail.

They also took with them an offering of three fat mice as a present for Old Brown, and put them down upon his door-step.

Then Twinkleberry and the other little squirrels each made a low bow, and said politely —

"Old Mr. Brown, will you favour us with permission to gather nuts upon your island?"

But Nutkin was excessively impertinent in his manners. He bobbed up and down like a little red *cherry*, singing —

"Riddle me, riddle me, rot-tot-tote
  A little wee man, in a red red coat
  A staff in his hand, and a stone in
    his throat;
  If you'll tell me this riddle, I'll give
    you a groat."

Now this riddle is as old as the hills; Mr. Brown paid no attention whatever to Nutkin.

He shut his eyes obstinately and went to sleep.

The squirrels filled their little sacks with nuts,
and sailed away home in the evening.

But next morning they all came back again to Owl Island; and Twinkleberry and the others brought a fine fat mole, and laid it on the stone in front of Old Brown's doorway, and said —

"Mr. Brown, will you favour us with your gracious permission to gather some more nuts?"

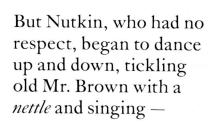

But Nutkin, who had no respect, began to dance up and down, tickling old Mr. Brown with a *nettle* and singing —

"Old Mr. B! Riddle-me-ree!
Hitty Pitty within the wall,
Hitty Pitty without the wall;
If you touch Hitty Pitty,
Hitty Pitty will bite you!"

Mr. Brown woke up suddenly and carried the mole into his house.

He shut the door in Nutkin's face. Presently a little thread of blue *smoke* from a wood fire came up from the top of the tree, and Nutkin peeped through the key-hole and sang —

"A house full, a hole full!
  And you cannot gather a bowl-full!"

The squirrels searched for nuts all over the island and filled their little sacks.

But Nutkin gathered oak-apples — yellow and scarlet —and sat upon a beech-stump playing marbles, and watching the door of old Mr. Brown.

On the third day the squirrels got up very early and went fishing; they caught seven fat minnows as a present for Old Brown.

They paddled over the lake and landed under a crooked chestnut tree on Owl Island.

Twinkleberry and six other little squirrels each carried a fat minnow; but Nutkin, who had no nice manners, brought no present at all. He ran in front, singing —

"The man in the wilderness
     said to me,
'How many strawberries grow
     in the sea?'
I answered him as I thought
     good—
'As many red herrings as grow
     in the wood.' "

But old Mr. Brown took no interest in riddles — not even when the answer was provided for him.

On the fourth day the squirrels brought a present of six fat beetles, which were as good as plums in *plum-pudding* for Old Brown. Each beetle was wrapped up carefully in a dock-leaf, fastened with a pine-needle pin.

But Nutkin sang as rudely as ever —

"Old Mr. B! Riddle-me-ree!
  flour of England, fruit of Spain,
  Met together in a shower of rain;
  Put in a bag tied round with a string,
  If you'll tell me this riddle, I'll give you a ring!"

Which was ridiculous of Nutkin, because he had not got any ring to give to Old Brown.

The other squirrels hunted up and down the nut bushes; but Nutkin gathered robin's pin-cushions off a briar bush, and stuck them full of pine-needle pins.

On the fifth day the
squirrels brought a
present of wild honey;
it was so sweet and sticky
that they licked their
fingers as they put it
down upon the stone.
They had stolen it out
of a bumble *bees*' nest
on the tippitty top of
the hill.

But Nutkin skipped up
and down, singing —

"Hum-a-bum! buzz! buzz! Hum-a-bum buzz!
  As I went over Tipple-tine
  I met a flock of bonny swine;
  Some yellow-nacked, some yellow backed!
  They were the very bonniest swine
  That e'er went over Tipple-tine."

Old Mr. Brown turned up
his eyes in disgust at the
impertinence of Nutkin.
  But he ate up the honey!

The squirrels filled their little sacks with nuts.

But Nutkin sat upon a big flat rock, and played ninepins with a crab apple and green fir-cones.

On the sixth day, which was Saturday, the squirrels came again for the last time; they brought a new-laid *egg* in a little rush basket as a last parting present for Old Brown.

But Nutkin ran in front laughing, and shouting—

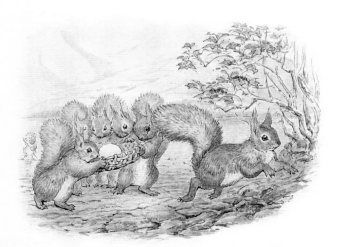

"Humpty Dumpty lies in
    the beck,
With a white counterpane
    round his neck,
Forty doctors and forty wrights,
Cannot put Humpty Dumpty
    to rights!"

Now old Mr. Brown took an interest in eggs; he opened one eye and shut it again. But still he did not speak.

Nutkin became more and more impertinent —

"Old Mr. B! Old Mr. B!
  Hickamore, Hackamore,
    on the King's kitchen door;
  All the King's horses,
    and all the King's men,
  Couldn't drive Hickamore,
    Hackamore,
  Off the King's kitchen door!"

Nutkin danced up and down like a *sunbeam*; but still Old Brown said nothing at all.

Nutkin began again —

"Arthur O'Bower has broken
his band,
He comes roaring up the land
The King of Scots with all
his power,
Cannot turn Arthur of the
Bower!"

Nutkin made a whirring noise to sound like the *wind*, and he took a running jump right onto the head of Old Brown! . . .

Then all at once there was a flutterment and a scufflement and a loud "Squeak!"

The other squirrels scuttered away into the bushes.

When they came back very cautiously, peeping round the tree — there was Old Brown sitting on his door-step, quite still, with his eyes closed, as if nothing had happened.

*

But Nutkin was in his waist-coat pocket!

This looks like the end of the story; but it isn't.

Old Brown carried Nutkin into his house, and held him up by the tail, intending to skin him; but Nutkin pulled so very hard that his tail broke in two, and he dashed up the staircase, and escaped out of the attic window.

And to this day, if you meet Nutkin up a tree and ask him
a riddle, he will throw sticks at you, and stamp his feet and
scold, and shout —
    "Cuck-cuck-cuck-cur-r-r-cuck-k-k!"

The End,

of the tale AND the tail, so to speak!

Or was it?

Mr. Brown,
Owl Island.

Sir,
I should esteem it a favour if you would
let me have back my tail, as I miss it
very much. I would pay postage.

Yrs. truly,
Squirrel Nutkin.

Mr. Old Brown Esq.,
Owl Island.

Dear Sir,
I should be extremely obliged if you
could kindly send back a tail which you
have had for some time. It is fluffy
brown with a white tip. I wrote to you
before about it, but perhaps I did not
address the letter properly. I will pay
the postage.

Yrs. respectfully,
Sq. Nutkin.

The Right Honourable
Old Brown Esq;,
Owl Island.

Sir,
I write respectfully to beg that you
will sell me back my tail, I am so
uncomfortable without it, and I have
heard of a tailor who would sew it on
again. I would pay three bags of
nuts for it. Please Sir, Mr. Brown, send it
back by post & oblige.

Yrs. respectfully,
Sq. Nutkin.

O. Brown Esq., M.P.
Owl Island.

Dear Sir,
I write on behalf of my brother Nutkin to
beg that as a great favour you would send
him back his tail. He never makes - or asks -
riddles now, and he is truly sorry that he
was so rude. Trusting that you continue to
enjoy good health, I remain,

Yr. obedient servant,
Twinkleberry Squirrel.

Master Squirrel Nutkin,
Derwent Bay Wood.

Mr. Brown writes to say that he cannot reply to letters as he is asleep. Mr. Brown cannot return the tail. He ate it some time ago; it nearly choked him. Mr. Brown requests Nutkin not to write again, as his repeated letters are a nuisance.

Dr. Maggotty,
The Dispensary.

Dear Dr. Maggotty,
Having seen an advertisement (nailed on the smithy door) of your blue beans to cure chilblains, I write to ask whether you think a boxful would make my tail grow? I tried to buy it back from the gentleman who pulled it off, but he has not answered my letters. It spoils my appearance. Are the beans very strong?

Yrs. truly,
Sq. Nutkin..

Sq. Nutkin Esq.,
Derwent Bay Wood.

Sir,

I have much pleasure in
forwarding a box of blue beans
as requested.
Kindly acknowledge receipt &
send 30 peppercorns as payment.

Yrs.
Matthew Maggotty, M.D.

Dr. Maggotty Esq, M.D.
The Dispensary.

Sir,

I am obliged for the box of blue
beans. I have not tried them yet.
I have been wondering is there
any fear they might make me
grow a blue tail? It would spoil my
appearance.

Yrs. truly,
Sq. Nutkin.

Sq. Nutkin Esq.,
Derwent Bay Wood.

Sir,

I do not think that there is the slightest risk of my beans causing you to grow a blue tail. The price per box is 30 peppercorns.

Yrs. truly,
M. Maggotty, M.D.

POST CARD

FOR CORRESPONDENCE

FOR ADDRESS

ILFRACOMBE
1 -PM
9 SEP
1958
DEVON

Sir,
I am sending back the box of blue beans, I think they have a very funny smell & so does my brother Twinkleberry.

Yrs. truly,
Sq. Nutkin

Dr. Maggotty Esq,
The Dispensary.

TAKE HEED!

*T*hat squirrel Nutkin really is a cheeky young creature! I can't imagine what got into him – how could he have been so rude? Unlike his polite friends, Nutkin danced about and teased Old Brown with his silly sing-song riddles – not once, but six times! No wonder the elderly owl lost his temper, especially when Nutkin jumped upon his head! That young squirrel really needs to learn some manners. And I'm sure that from now on, Nutkin will show some respect for those older and wiser than himself!

Now Nutkin finds himself the only squirrel in the woods with half a tail, and rather a joke among his friends. Needless to say, he no longer tells riddles and he has never been seen on Owl Island since. Has the naughty squirrel learnt his lesson? Let us hope so!

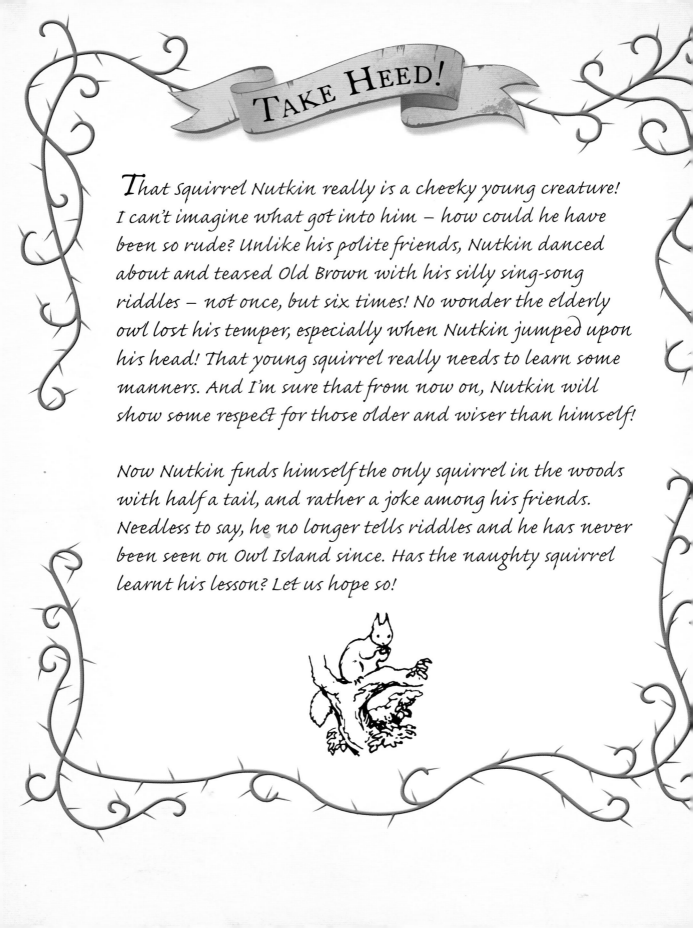

THE END

At last we have come to the end of our tales.
Weren't those creatures the most
badly behaved animals that ever lived?

But wait . . . who is this?

Could there be ANOTHER creature
that is even more badly behaved?
I am sorry to say that there is!

THE STORY OF
A FIERCE BAD RABBIT

Well, what more can we say?

ABOUT THIS BOOK

The Story of A Fierce Bad Rabbit, together with *The Story of Miss Moppet*, was first published as a panorama, unfolding in a long strip of pictures and text from a wallet with a tuck-in flap. Both books were intended for very young children; *The Story of A Fierce Bad Rabbit* had been written especially for editor Harold Warne's little daughter, Louie, who had told Beatrix that Peter was too good a rabbit, and she wanted a story about a *really* naughty one!

Unfortunately the panoramic format was not popular with the bookshops. As Beatrix wrote later: "The shops sensibly refused to stock them because they got unrolled and so bad to roll up again." In 1916, both stories were reprinted in book form and listed at the end of the series of Peter Rabbit books, alongside the nursery rhyme collections which were also intended for the very young.

THIS IS A FIERCE BAD RABBIT; look at his savage whiskers, and his claws and his turned-up tail.

This is a nice gentle Rabbit. His mother has given him a carrot.

The bad Rabbit would like some carrot.

He doesn't say "Please." He takes it!

And he scratches the good Rabbit very badly.

The good Rabbit creeps away, and hides in a hole. It feels sad.

This is a man with a gun.

He sees something sitting on a bench. He thinks it is a very funny bird!

He comes creeping up behind the trees.

And then he shoots
— BANG!

This is what happens —

But this is all he finds on the bench, when he rushes up with his gun.

The good Rabbit peeps out of its hole.

And it sees the bad Rabbit tearing past — without any tail or whiskers!

Thank goodness, it's THE END!

I'm sure you are as shocked as me to hear about the behavior of the Fierce Bad Rabbit. Wasn't he fierce – and so very, very bad! How dreadful to take what belongs to someone else, and to scratch them too! I think you'll agree that this bullying bunny got exactly what he deserved …

So if you ever spot a rather grumpy-looking rabbit in your garden, one who is missing a tail and whiskers, you will know it is the Fierce Bad Rabbit himself. And I hope, dear readers, that you will remember how he – and all the other animals in our tales – were punished for their naughtiness. So remember to be good, just like the well-behaved little rabbit in our last story, who has still got his lovely bunny tail and gleaming whiskers!

THE END

Yes, really.

No other creatures could

POSSIBLY be so naughty!